P9-CET-571

the Animal Rescue Club

story and pictures by
John Himmelman

HarperCollins*Publishers*

*For Anita, who saved some lives,
and changed some lives*

HarperCollins®, 🐾®, and I Can Read Book® are trademarks of HarperCollins Publishers Inc.

The Animal Rescue Club
Copyright © 1998 by John Himmelman
Manufactured in China. All rights reserved.
For information address HarperCollins Children's
Books, a division of HarperCollins Publishers,
10 East 53rd Street, New York, NY 10022.

Library of Congress Cataloging-in-Publication Data
Himmelman, John.
  The Animal Rescue Club / story and pictures by John Himmelman.
    p.   cm.
  "I can read Chapter book."
  Summary: Members of the Animal Rescue Club save wild animals in trouble, nurse
them back to health, and return them to the wild.
  ISBN 0-06-027408-5. — ISBN 0-06-027409-3 (lib. bdg.) — ISBN 0-06-444224-1 (pbk.)
  [1. Wildlife rescue—Fiction.   2. Clubs—Fiction.]   I. Title.
PZ7.H5686An   1998   96-37987
[Fic]—dc21   CIP
                                                                                        AC

13 14 15 16 17 SCP 20 19 18 17 16 15 14
❖

Visit us on the World Wide Web!
http://www.harperchildrens.com

Contents

1. Stuck in the Mud   5

2. Down the Drain   15

3. Around and Around   27

4. Teamwork   37

5. Hanging by a Tail   41

Chapter 1
Stuck in the Mud

Jeffrey was soaking wet. He was riding his bike home in the rain, and the tires were sticking in the mud. He pedaled harder. Suddenly he heard a shout.

"Hey!" A boy waved to Jeffrey from the edge of a big mud puddle. A girl had waded into the middle of it. "Could you give us a hand?" the boy asked Jeffrey.

"What are you doing?" Jeffrey asked.

"A squirrel is stuck in the mud," the boy said. "My friend is trying to rescue it. My job is to get help if she gets stuck."

The girl picked up a muddy squirrel. Then she slipped.

"Help!" she called. "I'm stuck."

"Here's your help," shouted the boy. He patted Jeffrey's back. "Would you go help her?" he asked. "I don't like mud puddles. I read a story about a boy who sank into one all the way up to his nose. He didn't get out for days."

"I'll go," said Jeffrey.

The mud was very deep. Jeffrey walked carefully.

"Here, take the squirrel," said the girl. "Be gentle, but don't drop it."

Jeffrey took the squirrel. The girl pushed herself up and followed him. One of her boots was lost in the mud.

"I hate wearing boots anyway," she said, and grinned at Jeffrey. "Thanks for your help. I'm Beaner and this is Raymond."

Jeffrey told them his name and asked, "Is the squirrel okay?"

"It is breathing all right," Raymond said. He wrapped the squirrel in a towel. "This is a Gray Squirrel. They can swim, but not in mud."

Beaner took off her other boot and tucked the squirrel inside. "This will keep it dry for the ride," she said.

"Where are you taking it?" Jeffrey asked.

"To a hospital for wild animals," said Raymond.

"Wow," said Jeffrey. "Can I come?"

"Follow us," said Beaner.

Beaner and Raymond led Jeffrey to the hospital. A woman named Anita was cleaning a cage, and a boy named Mike was feeding a raccoon with a baby bottle. Anita took the squirrel from Beaner.

"This squirrel is very weak," Anita said. "We will clean her up and let her get some rest. What should we name her?"

"How about Mudpie?" suggested Jeffrey.

"Perfect," said Anita.

"The raccoon's name is Nikki," said Mike. "She lost her mother."

"Now we are her mothers," said Beaner.

"And fathers!" said Raymond. "This is the Animal Rescue Club. We rescue wild animals that are hurt and help them get better."

"Then we set them free," said Mike.

"Want to join, Jeffrey?" Beaner asked. "We can always use more help."

"Sounds great!" said Jeffrey.

Chapter 2
Down the Drain

The next day Jeffrey went back to the Animal Rescue Club.

"Mudpie is doing better," Anita said, "but she still needs rest. Another call just came in. We need an opossum rescue on Maple Street."

"Grab your bike, Jeffrey," Beaner said.

"I don't know what to do," said Jeffrey.

"We will tell you," said Raymond.

"Can I ride with you, Jeffrey?" Mike asked. "Beaner hits all the bumps in the road, and Raymond wobbles too much."

"Don't you have a bike?" asked Jeffrey.

"I don't see well," said Mike. "Since I can only make out shapes and shadows, I can't steer a bike."

"Oh," said Jeffrey. "Sure, you can ride with me."

"Come on, guys!" said Beaner.

The Animal Rescue Club raced to Maple Street.

"The opossum is up on the roof," a man said. "It got stuck in the drainpipe."

"Only a baby opossum would fit in a drainpipe," said Mike.

"It should be asleep now," Raymond said. "Opossums are night animals."

"I will get a ladder," the man said.

"Where's Beaner?" asked Jeffrey.

"I'm on the roof," called Beaner.

"How did you get up there?" Jeffrey asked.

"I climbed," Beaner said.

"Beaner isn't afraid of anything," said Raymond.

The man came back with a ladder.

"Why don't you go up," Raymond said to Jeffrey. "I don't like high places. I read a story about a man who climbed to the top of a ladder. His legs shook so much that the ladder fell apart."

Mike held out a pair of thick gloves. "Wear these," he said.

"Opossums can bite," Raymond said. "I read a story—"

"Don't tell me," said Jeffrey. He put on the gloves and climbed up the ladder. He tried to keep his legs from shaking.

"The opossum is really stuck," said
Beaner. "I don't want to pull any harder."

"I have an idea," Jeffrey said. He
pulled the pipe off the gutter and pushed
the little opossum out.

22

"Got him!" said Beaner. "Now you take him down. I will slide the drainpipe back."

"Gutters are for raindrops, not for opossums," Jeffrey said. The opossum sniffed his ear. Jeffrey jumped, and the ladder wobbled.

"Help!" cried Jeffrey.

Beaner grabbed Jeffrey's shirt. "Got you!" she said.

The man and Raymond grabbed the ladder. "It's steady now," they called.

"Thanks, Beaner," Jeffrey said.

"You helped me yesterday. I helped you today," she said. "Let's get the opossum back to the hospital."

Chapter 3
Around and Around

They named the opossum Raindrop. He was skinny, but he did not want to eat.

"Raindrop is scared," Anita said. "He has a lot of new smells and sounds to get used to. It will take time."

Mudpie was sitting up and eating. "You look great!" Jeffrey told her.

"She is ready to go back to the wild," Anita said.

"Let's take her," said Raymond.

"I'm going to stay here," Mike said. "Raindrop needs me."

Jeffrey, Beaner, and Raymond took Mudpie to the place they had found her.

"Good luck, Mudpie," Jeffrey said. "Stay out of mud puddles."

Mudpie climbed onto his shoulder.

"She's not leaving!" he said.

"Squirrels feel safer up in trees," said Raymond. "You're the next best thing."

Jeffrey walked to a tree. Mudpie jumped to it and ran up the trunk. Another squirrel met her, and the two ran across the branches.

"Be careful up there!" Jeffrey called.

"That's how squirrels should act," Beaner said. "Good luck, Mudpie!"

Back at the hospital, they told Anita and Mike about Mudpie's new friend.

"Mike has good news too," Anita said.

"Raindrop likes grapes!" Mike said. "I gave him food that was fun to touch, and now he's eating."

"We need another rescue," Anita said. "We just got a call about a goose in trouble on Catfish Lake."

Jeffrey, Beaner, and Raymond took off again.

At the edge of the lake, a goose was spinning around in circles.

"Geese aren't supposed to swim like that," Raymond said.

"The water isn't very deep," said Beaner. "We can wade in and chase it onto the land. Then we can grab it."

"I don't like lakes," said Raymond. "I read a story about fish who nibble at your toes. I will wait here."

Beaner and Jeffrey waded into the water. Jeffrey kept an eye out for fish. They shouted at the goose and splashed water. But the goose didn't swim out of the lake. The goose flew out of the lake.

"Help!" yelled Raymond. "It's after me!" He ran to a tree. The goose limped after him.

Beaner grabbed the goose. The goose grabbed Beaner. "It's got my hair," Beaner cried. Jeffrey tried to pull the goose away.

"Ouch!" said Beaner.

"It won't let go," Jeffrey said.

"Hold its head so it can't grab my ear," said Beaner. "I will have to carry it like this."

The goose held on to Beaner's hair all the way back to the hospital.

Chapter 4
Teamwork

"One of the goose's feet is normal," said Anita. "But the other is closed up tight."

"Then it can use only one foot when it swims," Raymond said. "That must be why it was spinning in circles."

Anita said, "Mike, you have smart fingers. Can you feel if the foot is broken?"

Mike felt the feet carefully. "The bones feel the same to me," he said.

"Then the problem must be the muscles," said Anita. "They weren't strong enough to hold the foot open. So it grew closed instead."

"Can we make the goose a special shoe?" Mike asked. "It could hold the foot open so the muscles grow properly."

"I have an idea," Jeffrey said. He rolled a piece of paper into a ball and put it into the goose's closed foot. "This will hold the foot open a little," he said. "We can tape a bigger ball in place every week. We'll stop when the foot stays open by itself."

"Great idea!" said Anita. "Good work, Jeffrey and Mike."

Mike grinned. "We make a pretty good team."

"I have the perfect name for the goose," Beaner said. "Dizzy!"

Chapter 5
Hanging by a Tail

The Animal Rescue Club was busy during the next few weeks. Nikki the raccoon grew big and fat. Raindrop grew fatter, too, but Mike was still worried about him.

"Opossums are supposed to hang by their tails," said Mike. "Raindrop just sits on the floor."

"Come help us with Dizzy, Mike," said Anita. "It's time to take the final bandage off his foot."

Anita cut the bandage and took away the ball of paper.

"Dizzy's foot is staying open!" Raymond cried.

"Let me feel," said Mike. He felt Dizzy's good foot. Then he felt the other one. "They feel the same!" he said.

"Take him to the lake," said Anita. "See if his feet work in water."

They took Dizzy to Catfish Lake. Dizzy put his head under the water and spun around.

"Oh, no!" said Jeffrey. "It didn't work."

Then Dizzy lifted his head. His mouth was full of weeds.

"He was just eating," Raymond said.

Dizzy honked and swam to join the other geese.

"He's fine," said Beaner. "We did it!"

45

Back at the hospital, Raindrop was hanging by his tail.

"Hey!" said Jeffrey. "How did he learn to do that?"

"I just took his tail and wrapped it around the branch," said Mike. "Now he knows how to do it."

"Sometimes all we need is for someone to take our hand. Or tail," said Anita. "A call came in. A rabbit is stuck under a porch on Elm Street."

"Let's go," Beaner said. "Mike, will Raindrop be okay without you now?"

"I know he will," said Mike.

And the Animal Rescue Club raced off to another rescue.

Author's Note

Rescuing wild animals can be exciting and fun. But it can also be dangerous. Many animals that seem friendly can bite, scratch, or carry a disease. If you ever find an animal that looks injured, *stay away!* Tell an adult and have that person call a local nature center or the Department of Environmental Protection.

Do not try to take care of wild animals on your own. In many states it is against the law to keep wild animals in cages, even if they are injured and you are trying to help them. A person must have a license to do this. People who help orphaned and injured animals are called Wildlife Rehabilitators. Anita in this story is based on a real person. Like other Wildlife Rehabilitators, she took many classes in working with wild animals and received extensive training. The children who helped her also had to be trained before they were allowed to work with the animals.

If you would like to learn more about helping wildlife, call a local nature center and volunteer to help!